rescues HALLOWEEN

DEC 1977

PARENTS' MAGAZINE PRESS/NEW YORK

Copyright © 1972 by Wende and Harry Devlin
All rights reserved
Printed in the United States of America

Library of Congress Cataloging in Publication Data
Devlin, Wende.
  Old Witch rescues Halloween!
  SUMMARY : Old Witch uses her magic to overcome
Mr. Butterbean's edict against Halloween.

  [1. Halloween—Stories] I. Devlin, Harry,
joint author. II. Title.
PZ7.D4990n   [E]   72-676
ISBN 0-8193-0608-8   ISBN 0-8193-0609-6 (lib. bdg.)

OLD WITCH

For Heather

RESCUES HALLOWEEN

WENDE and HARRY DEVLIN

Old Witch sat cracking black walnuts in the attic of the old Jug and Muffin Tearoom. The nights were growing colder and the smells of apples and cornstalks filled the winds.

Only one more night until Halloween! One night! Old Witch's eyes glowed brighter. Every once in a while she hopped about in a stiff little witch's jig.

Point your toe,
skip and prance.
It's Halloween
and time to dance.

But now she stopped! Downstairs she heard a door bang. It was Nicky.

She knew it was Nicky. Ever since the night that he and his mother had found her fast asleep in the chimney of the lonely old house, Nicky had been her friend. And she knew by the way the door slammed that something was wrong.

"Old Witch! Old Witch!" Nicky called. Old Witch heard the alarm in Nicky's voice. Down the stairs she clattered to join the breathless boy and his mother.

"It's Mr. Butterbean. Mr. Butterbean chased me!" he gasped. "He chased me with a stick. He smashed my pumpkin!"

Nicky faced Old Witch and his voice began to shake. "Mr. Butterbean said *there won't be any Halloween in Oldwick tomorrow night!*"

No Halloween?

Nicky's mother, Nicky and Old Witch stared at one another. They couldn't believe their ears! They knew that Mr. Butterbean was mean—they knew he chased children and they also knew that people usually did what he told them to do because he owned most of the town of Oldwick.

"He's going down to Town Meeting tonight and tell the mayor that there will be *no Halloween in Oldwick*," said Nicky.

Old Witch cracked her knuckles and rolled her eyes. Suddenly she turned and clattered back upstairs.

"Poor Old Witch. She loves Halloween," said Nicky.

"Poor dear Old Witch. Halloween is her night," said Nicky's mother.

Upstairs, Old Witch crashed about. From under her bed she pulled a tin box of strange red powder. From an earthen crock she took a hank of hair and from behind a beam she took three dried seeds.

Cackling wickedly, she tucked them away in her cape
and sang a little song.

Snakes' knees, toads, and ratchafratch.
Old Butterbean has met his match!

She winked at the crow outside her window.

In Oldwick, Mr. Butterbean let everyone know what he planned to do at Town Hall that night.

The bad news spread fast and all day the people of Oldwick worried that Mr. Butterbean would do just what he said he would do. They worried that there wouldn't be a Halloween. At dusk, as the town lights came on, unhappy children and their anxious parents began to gather early at Town Hall.

Nicky and his mother quickly cleaned up the tearoom so they could be at the meeting in time. Old Witch, scowling angrily, scooted on ahead. She took her favorite shortcut through the woods, past the great house called Butterbean Manor. The moon was beginning to rise, but the path was dark.

In front of the mansion a crow called an alarm and
Old Witch stopped. She cupped an ear to catch the
warning.

Too late! Too late! *Whoosh! Swish!* and a blanket was thrown over her. Kicking and screeching, she was bundled off to Butterbean Manor and up the stairs to a room high in the tower. Before she could fight her way out of the blanket, she heard a key locking the door.

Spluttering, Old Witch made her way to the window and flung it open. Far below she saw Mr. Butterbean drive off to the meeting at Town Hall.

"Snakes' knees!" she rasped. "My broom, I'll fly down." Where was her broom? It must be back on the path, she thought. For a moment it seemed that all was lost. But only for a moment.

Old Witch leaned out of the window and whistled. The great black crow that never seemed to be very far from her flew to the sill. Old Witch, with a whispered word, sent the huge crow swooping into the woods.

In a moment, he came struggling back clutching the broom in his beak.

"Beautiful bird!" she squawked. And now, perched on her broom, Old Witch soared out of the window towards the Town Hall.

In the center of town, the meeting had begun. Mr. Butterbean was shaking his cane at the crowd. Beside him on the platform, Oldwick's mayor looked very upset.

"Down with Halloween," shouted Butterbean.

"Down with noisy children.

"Down with trick or treats!

"There will be NO Halloween in Oldwick this year!"

"But-but-but, Mr. Butterbean," squeaked the mayor, wiping his glasses unhappily.

"No Halloween!" Butterbean thundered.

Some children began to cry. Where was Old Witch? After all, Halloween was really her night! Where was she?

At that moment there was a *whirr*, a *swish* and an angry squawk at the open window.

And in sailed Old Witch, trailing a lace curtain from Butterbean Manor! She flew over the heads of the people and straight to the speakers' platform, knocking off hats and overturning chairs on the way.

The children shrieked with joy!

Old Witch came to a screeching stop in front of Mr. Butterbean.

Mr. Butterbean could hardly believe his eyes. He stared in amazement at Old Witch. How could she have escaped from the tower? Then his fury returned. He snatched a pitcher of water from the speakers' table and dumped it on Old Witch. "Troublemaker!" he shouted.

For a moment Old Witch just dripped.

And then, with water squishing in her shoes, she broke
into a furious jig—her eyes glittered and she hissed:

Spiders, snakes' knees
and witches' grog.
Butterbean
is a bright green frog!

While Butterbean continued his shouting, Old Witch reached into her cape and threw a powder into the air. In the middle of a shout, Mr. Butterbean changed. He wanted to say, "Down with Halloween," but it came out, "Down with ... GROINK!

"Groink?" he asked himself.

"Groink?" asked the mayor.

"Groink?" asked the audience.

"Groink," said Mr. Butterbean. It was a very small "groink" because suddenly Mr. Butterbean was a very small frog.

No one could even see him at Old Witch's feet.

All they knew was that Old Witch was here and had taken charge.

"All right," she squawked, "all those in favor of a spooky, scary Halloween, say, *snakes' knees.*"

"SNAKES' KNEES!" shouted the crowd.

"All those in favor of cider and doughnuts say, *ratchafratch.*"

"RATCHAFRATCH!" they roared.

Then Old Witch bent down and seemed to mumble something to her feet.

There was a flash, a puff of smoke, and there stood Mr. Butterbean again. With a fearful look at Old Witch, he said, weakly, "Hurrah for Halloween!"

"Hurrah for Butterbean!" shouted someone.

"Hurrah for Old Witch!" shouted everyone.

Halloween was a clear, frosty blue night, and the moon rose full and orange. Children dressed in wonderful ghost and pirate costumes, scared one another and gathered treats until their bags were overflowing.

Even at Mr. Butterbean's house there were plates of sugar doughnuts, sweet apple cider and spicy pumpkin pies.

Old Witch stopped in for a moment to test the cider. She might have stayed longer if some children, visiting from out of town, hadn't pulled on her nose.

"Take off your mask," they said.

"Let's see your real face."

"Ratchafratch!" she squawked loudly and stamped out of the house.

The wind was in the trees and a black cat yowled.

"My night—Halloween," she cackled. And then, as though the sounds of night called, she rose into the dark blue skies.